MAD JUMBLE BOOK

by
Frank Jacobs
and
Bob Clarke

Edited by Albert B. Feldstein

WARNER BOOKS

A Warner Communications Company

CONTENTS

Words in Action 5

MAD Chimneys 31

One Day in Ancient Egypt 47

MADitions 55

Shapes the World is in 69

MAD Doors 81

The Idea Man 97

Sheet Music Roulette 109

Dates to Remember 121

Personalized Balloons 133

Insiders 143

On Account of a Dog 149

MAD Visits a Stock Broker's Office 161

Word Play 171

Distinctive Johns 183

Last Word..192

WORDS
IN
ACTION

THE PAST YEAR HAS SEEN THE FIRM IN A PE

...F CONSOLIDATION, WHICH IS THE MAIN REASON FOR THIS RATHE...

THE REAR OF THE BUS

THIS IS YOUR CAPTAIN SPEAKING... WE A

EXPERIENCING SOME MINOR MECHANICAL DIFFICULTIES, BUT I ASSURE YOU, THERE IS ABSOLUTELY NO CAUSE FOR ALARM

11

HAVERSHAM'S THEORY OF MOLECULAR

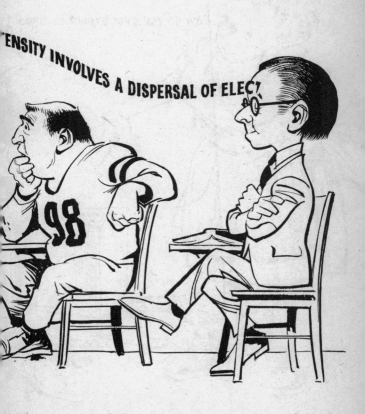

How do you ever expect to amount

14

15

17

THERE'S ONE *THING I HATE* IT'S DRIV*ING*

...N THE THRU*WAY DURING* RUSH HOUR

HOTCHKISS, JONES AND I WERE SCALING THE

...HEST PEAK WHEN SUDDENLY THE LINE SNAPPED! ...TOO BAD ABOUT GOOD OLD HOTCHKISS!

AT THE STRETCH IT'S CREEPY NICK BY A NOSE, FOLLOWED BY KNOCKWURST, THEN IT'S BILLY BOY

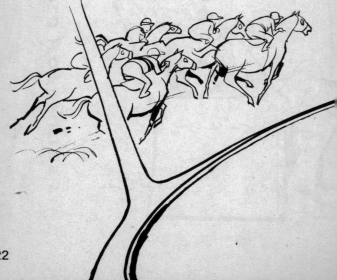

22

CLOSING IN ON THE OUTSIDE...

COMING INTO

25

MAD CHIMNEYS

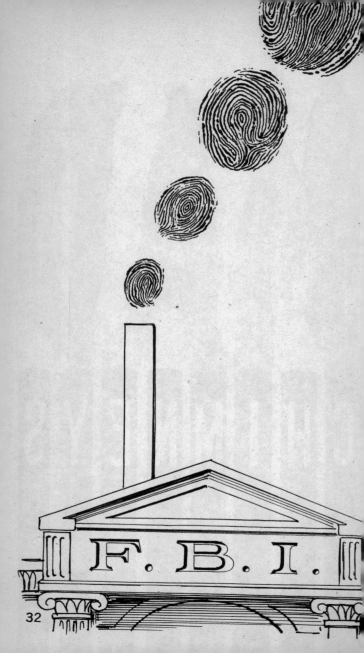

33

U.S. ROPE CO.

35

PLAYBOY PUBLICATIONS

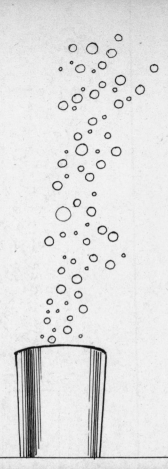

MILES LABORATORIES
makers of
Alka-Seltzer

ACE SECRETARIAL SCHOOL

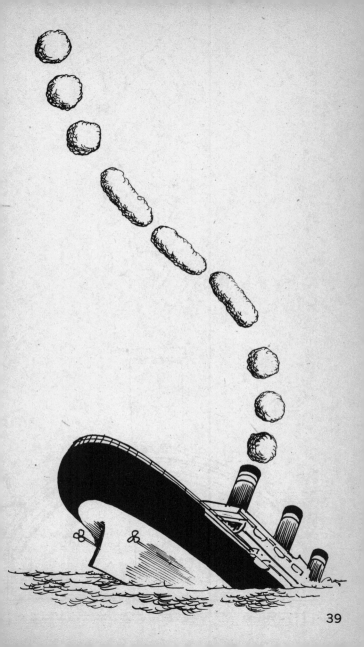

GOVERNMENT OFFICES:
UNION of SOUTH AFRICA

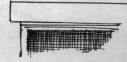

PLANNED PARENTHOOD
ASSOCIATION

43

THE NEW
REPUBLIC

THE
NATIONAL
REVIEW

44

EMBASSY OF
THE POLISH
PEOPLE'S
REPUBLIC

45

DEPARTMENT OF
**ENVIRONMENTAL
PROTECTION**

One day in ANCIENT EGYPT

49

51

52

53

M ADDITIONS

59

61

63

SHAPES
THE
WORLD
IS IN

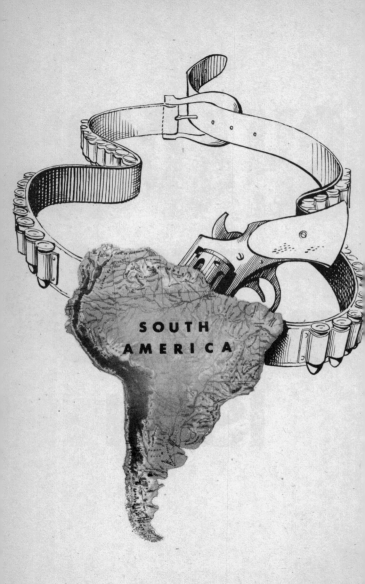

SOUTH AMERICA

ITALY

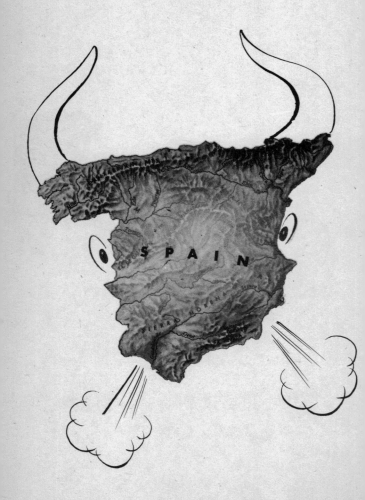

S P A I N

72

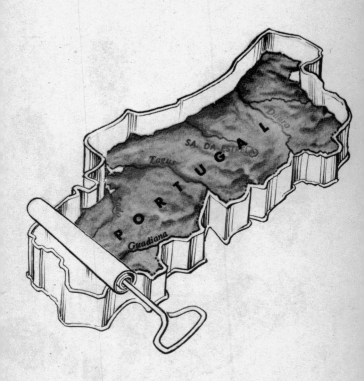

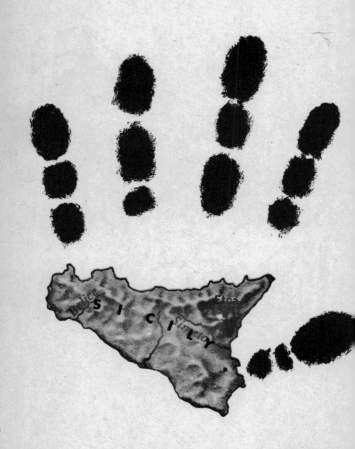

74

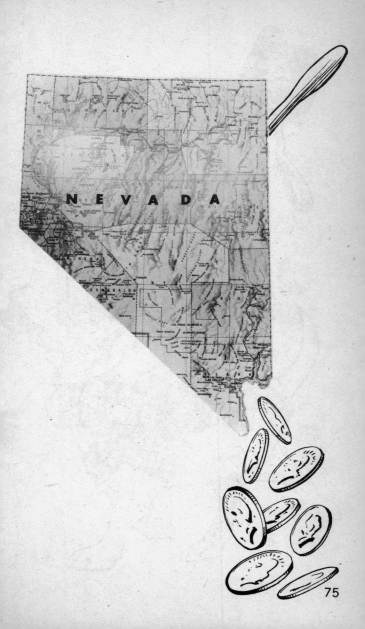

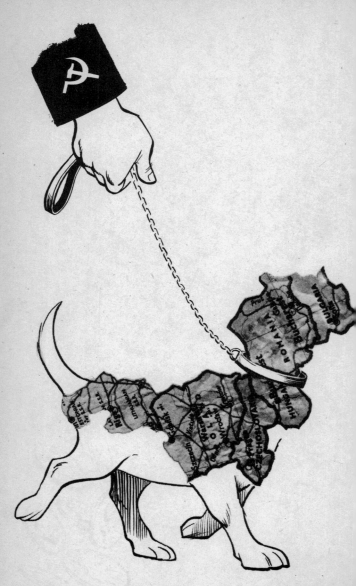

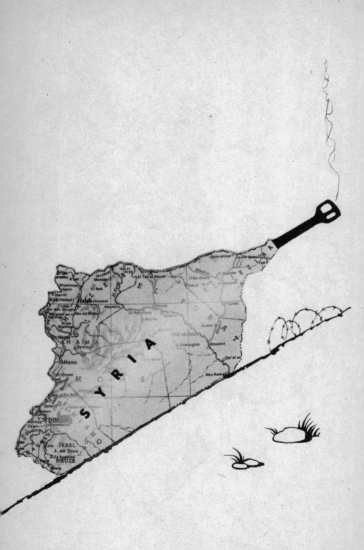

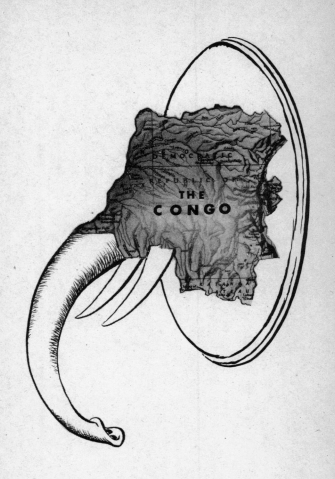

THE
CONGO

YING & YANG

KARATE
SCHOOL

CITY
TELEPHONE
COMPANY

TEMPORARILY
OUT OF SERVICE
Use Window

WEIGHT-WATCHERS
INCORPORATED

ENTRANCE

EXIT

SULLIVAN'S
TRUCK-DRIVING
SCHOOL

 YES

 NO

Embassy Of The Republic Of Germany

You VILL knock before entering!

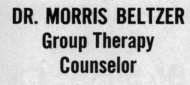

DR. MORRIS BELTZER
Group Therapy
Counselor

RAP

INSTITUTE
OF
PSYCHICAL
RESEARCH

KNOCK
BEFORE
MATERIALIZING

Taste Good
TAFFY COMPANY

PRODUCTS
DIVISION

P
U
L
L

Taste Good

TAFFY COMPANY

SALES
DIVISION

PUSH

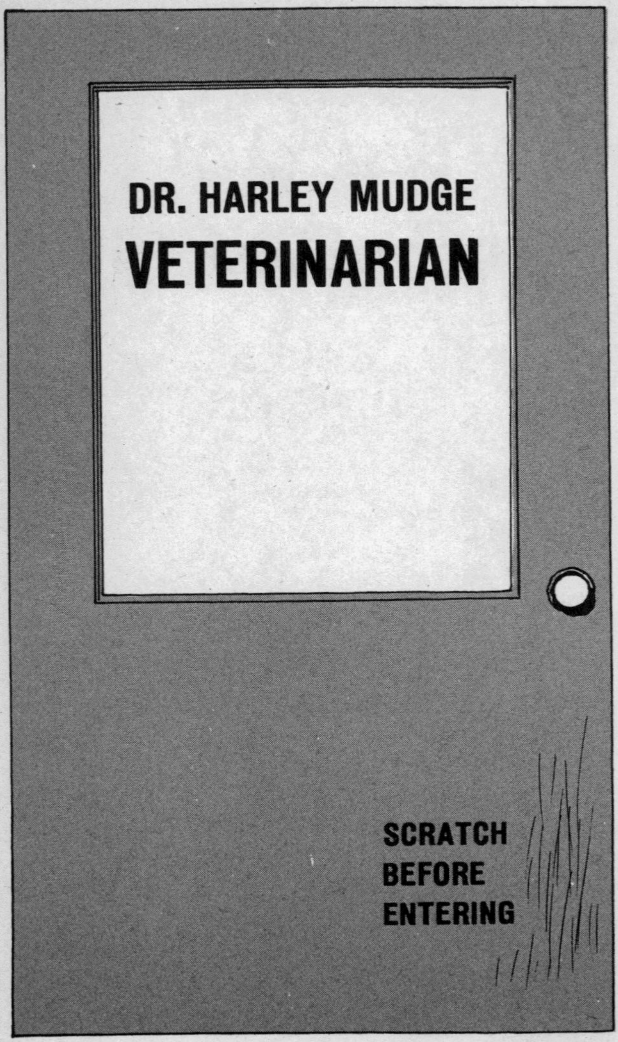

DR. HARLEY MUDGE
VETERINARIAN

SCRATCH
BEFORE
ENTERING

ACADEMY
OF
JAPANESE
LANGUAGE
STUDY

OUT TO RUNCH

EMBASSY
OF THE
POLISH PEOPLE'S
REPUBLIC

**Enter
THEN
knock**

MULLIGAN'S
TRAINING SCHOOL
FOR BOUNCERS

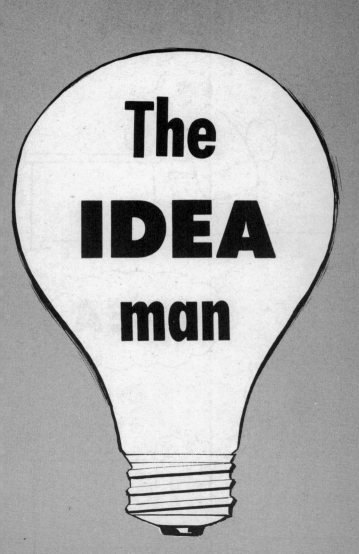

103

Sheet Music ROULETTE

Let's Do It

For
BURGLAR

TONIGHT

For All
We Know

AIN'T NOBODY HOME

It Ain't Necessarily So

What'll I Do?

I SURRENDER, DEAR

They Didn't Believe Me

I'M CONFESSIN'

In The Good Old
SUMMERTIME

For
MOTORIST

BUCKLE DOWN
WINSOCKI

In My Merry
OLDSMOBILE

114

Something's
Coming

MY WAY

FREIGHT
TRAIN

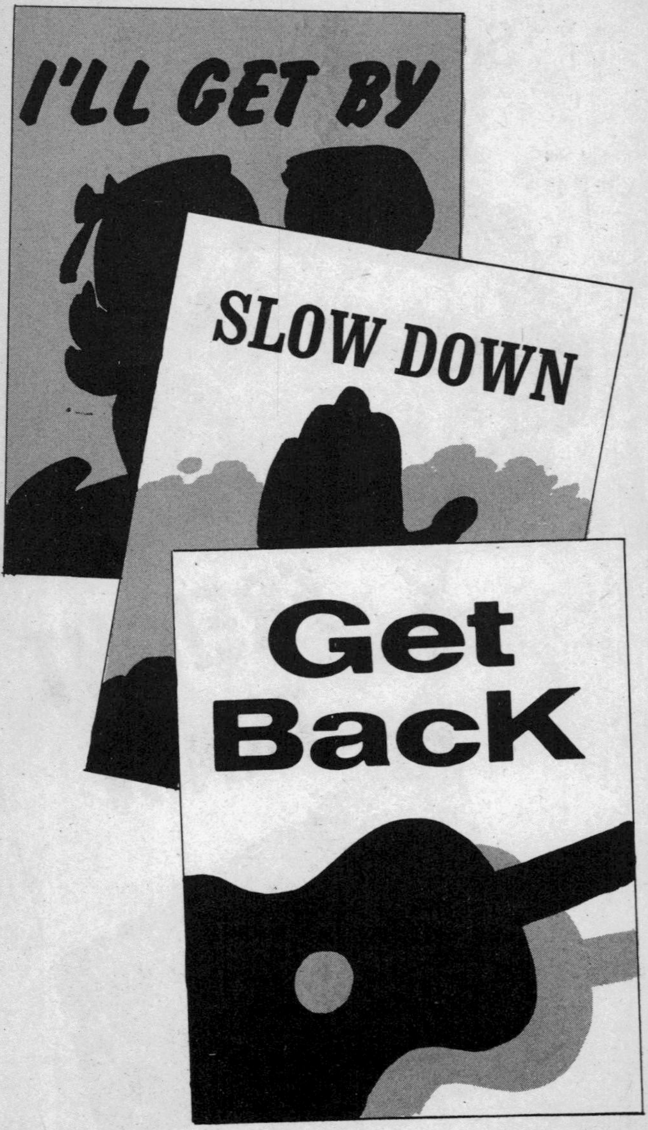
I'LL GET BY
SLOW DOWN
Get
Back

I CAN'T GET STARTED

HELP

Hark, the Herald Angels Sing

For INVESTORS

UP, UP, and AWAY

Everything's Coming Up Roses

THE TIMES WILL CHANGE

118

I SHOULD HAVE KNOWN BETTER

I'M DOWN

It's Impossible

119

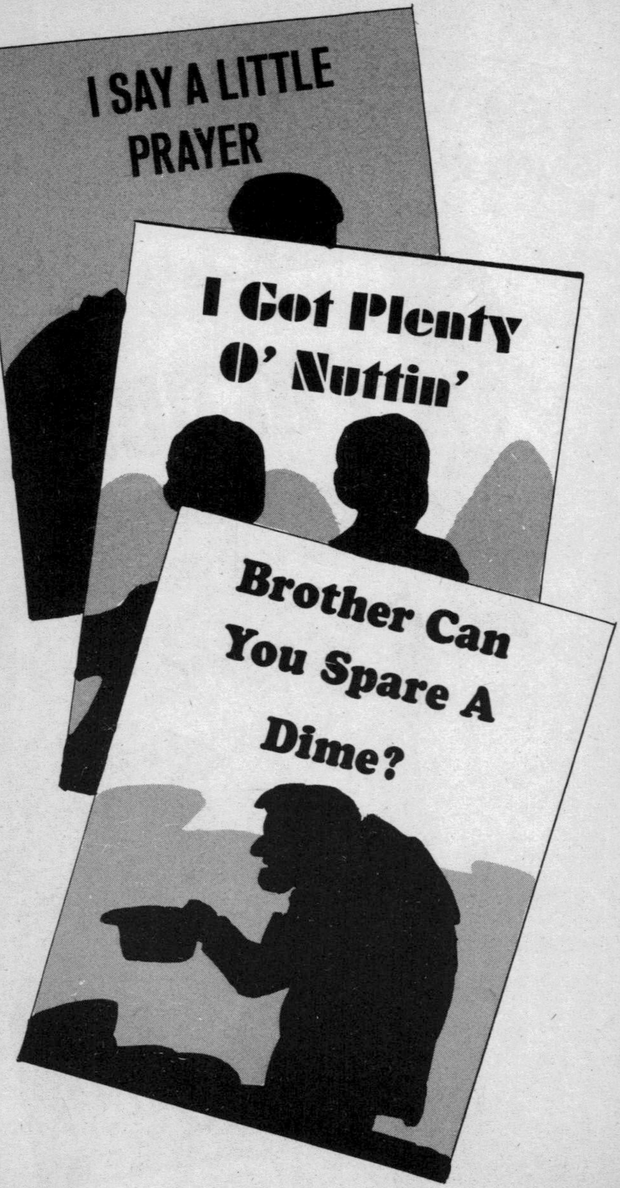

I SAY A LITTLE PRAYER

I Got Plenty O' Nuttin'

Brother Can You Spare A Dime?

DATES TO REMEMBER

125

131

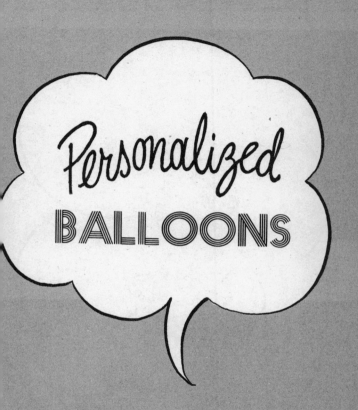

THE INTROVERT

HE BRAGGART

THE STUTTERER

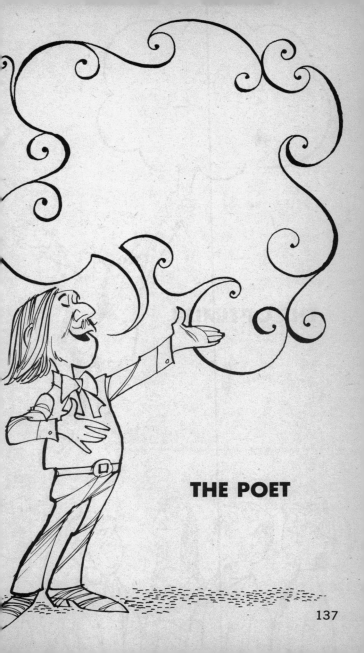

THE POET

THE OPTIMIST

THE PESSIMIST

139

THE CHAUVINIST

THE MILITARY MAN

THE BORE

144

145

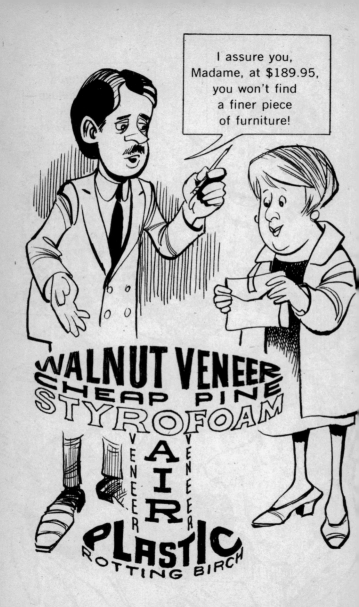

148

"On Account" of a Dog

MARVIN SCHMEER
FLOSSIE SCHMEER
41 ELM STREET
FINSTER, OHIO

No. 131

77-334
552

Aug 3 19 *74*

PAY TO THE ORDER OF *Sturdley Kennels* $ *165.00*

One Hundred Sixty-Five and 00/100 DOLLARS

FIRST NATIONAL BANK
25 MAIN STREET
FINSTER, OHIO

Marvin Schmeer

89⑈ ⑆02⑈46695⑈ 23010 3⑈05

MARVIN SCHMEER
FLOSSIE SCHMEER
41 ELM STREET
FINSTER, OHIO

No. 134

77-334
552

Aug 4 19 *74*

PAY TO THE ORDER OF *American Kennel Club Registry* $ *12.00*

Twelve and 00/100 DOLLARS

FIRST NATIONAL BANK
25 MAIN STREET
FINSTER, OHIO

Marvin Schmeer

89⑈ ⑆02⑈46695⑈ 23010 3⑈05

MARVIN SCHMEER
FLOSSIE SCHMEER
41 ELM STREET
FINSTER, OHIO

No. 135

77-334
552

Aug 4 19 *74*

PAY TO THE ORDER OF *County Licence Bureau* $ *6.00*

Six and 00/100 DOLLARS

FIRST NATIONAL BANK
25 MAIN STREET
FINSTER, OHIO

Marvin Schmeer

89⑈ ⑆02⑈46695⑈ 23010 3⑈05

MARVIN SCHMEER
FLOSSIE SCHMEER
41 ELM STREET
FINSTER, OHIO

Aug 5 19 74

No. 136

77-334
552

PAY TO THE
ORDER OF Woof-Woof Gourmet Shop $ 31.65

Thirty-One and 65/100 _____ DOLLARS

FIRST NATIONAL BANK
25 MAIN STREET
FINSTER, OHIO

Marvin Schmeer

⑂ ⑈:0 2 ⑈ 4 6 6 9 5 ⑈ 2 3 0 ⑈0 3 ⑈:0 5

MARVIN SCHMEER
FLOSSIE SCHMEER
41 ELM STREET
FINSTER, OHIO

No. 137

Aug 5 19 74

77-334
552

PAY TO THE
ORDER OF Swank Doggie Boutique $ 18.27

Eighteen and 27/100 _____ DOLLARS

FIRST NATIONAL BANK
25 MAIN STREET
FINSTER, OHIO

Marvin Schmeer

⑂ ⑈:0 2 ⑈ 4 6 6 9 5 ⑈ 2 3 0 ⑈0 3 ⑈:0 5

MARVIN SCHMEER
FLOSSIE SCHMEER
41 ELM STREET
FINSTER, OHIO

Sept 22 19 74

No. 165

77-334
552

PAY TO THE
ORDER OF Claude's Groom-a-Pup Salon $ 26.55

Twenty-Six and 55/100 _____ DOLLARS

FIRST NATIONAL BANK
25 MAIN STREET
FINSTER, OHIO

Marvin Schmeer

⑂ ⑈:0 2 ⑈ 4 6 6 9 5 ⑈ 2 3 0 ⑈0 3 ⑈:0 5

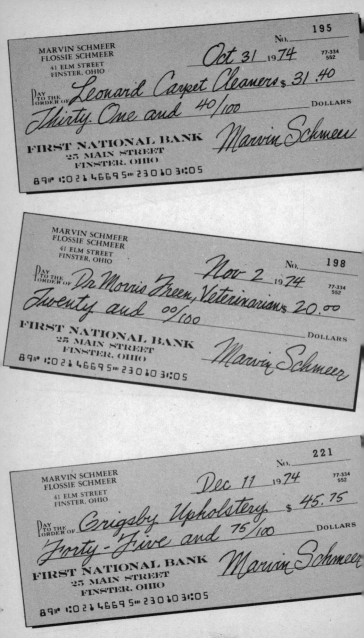

MARVIN SCHMEER
FLOSSIE SCHMEER
41 ELM STREET
FINSTER, OHIO

Dec. 15 1974   No. 226

77-334
552

PAY TO THE
ORDER OF Forbes Custom Drapery Cleaners $ 37.40

Thirty - Seven and 40/100 _____ DOLLARS

FIRST NATIONAL BANK
25 MAIN STREET
FINSTER, OHIO

Marvin Schmeer

89⑈ ⑆02⑈46695⑈230⑆03⑈05

MARVIN SCHMEER
FLOSSIE SCHMEER
41 ELM STREET
FINSTER, OHIO

No. 227

Dec. 16 1974   77-334
552

PAY TO THE
ORDER OF Happy Pup Obedience School $ 75.00

Seventy - Five and 00/100 _____ DOLLARS

FIRST NATIONAL BANK
25 MAIN STREET
FINSTER, OHIO

Marvin Schmeer

89⑈ ⑆02⑈46695⑈230⑆03⑈05

MARVIN SCHMEER
FLOSSIE SCHMEER
41 ELM STREET
FINSTER, OHIO

No. 245

Jan 8 1975   77-334
552

PAY TO THE
ORDER OF Daily Clarion Lost + Found $ 9.50

Nine and 50/100 _____

FIRST NATIONAL BANK
25 MAIN STREET
FINSTER, OHIO   DOLLARS

Marvin Schmeer

89⑈ ⑆02⑈46695⑈230⑆03⑈05

MARVIN SCHMEER
FLOSSIE SCHMEER
41 ELM STREET
FINSTER, OHIO

No. 247
77-334
552

Jan 10 19 75

PAY TO THE
ORDER OF Billy Smithers $ 10.00

Ten and 00/100   DOLLARS

FIRST NATIONAL BANK
25 MAIN STREET
FINSTER, OHIO

Marvin Schmeer

89"1:02146695"230103:05

MARVIN SCHMEER
FLOSSIE SCHMEER
41 ELM STREET
FINSTER, OHIO

No. 252
77-3
55.

Jan 18 19 75

PAY TO THE
ORDER OF Gallagher Oak Fence Co. $ 225.4

Two Hundred Twenty Five and 4/100 DOLLARS

FIRST NATIONAL BANK
25 MAIN STREET
FINSTER, OHIO

Marvin Schmeer

89"1:02146695"230103:05

MARVIN SCHMEER
FLOSSIE SCHMEER
41 ELM STREET
FINSTER, OHIO

No. 277
77-334
552

Feb. 10 19 75

PAY TO THE
ORDER OF Daily Clarion Lost & Found $ 9.50

Nine and 50/100   DOLLARS

FIRST NATIONAL BANK
25 MAIN STREET
FINSTER, OHIO

Marvin Schmeer

89"1:02146695"230103:05

MARVIN SCHMEER
FLOSSIE SCHMEER
41 ELM STREET
FINSTER, OHIO

No. 284

Feb. 13 19 75

77-334
552

PAY TO THE ORDER OF Daily Clarion Lost + Found $ 9.50

Nine and 50/100

DOLLARS

FIRST NATIONAL BANK
25 MAIN STREET
FINSTER, OHIO

Marvin Schmeer

89" ⑆02146695⑈23010 3⑆05

MARVIN SCHMEER
FLOSSIE SCHMEER
41 ELM STREET
FINSTER, OHIO

No. 287

Feb 16 19 75

77-334
552

PAY TO THE ORDER OF Tommy Cooper $ 10.00

Ten and 00/100

DOLLARS

FIRST NATIONAL BANK
25 MAIN STREET
FINSTER, OHIO

Marvin Schmeer

89" ⑆02146695⑈23010 3⑆05

MARVIN SCHMEER
FLOSSIE SCHMEER
41 ELM STREET
FINSTER, OHIO

No. 294

Feb. 21 19 75

77-334
552

PAY TO THE ORDER OF Steinberg Steel Fence Co. $ 345.50

Three Hundred Forty Five and 50/100 DOLLARS

FIRST NATIONAL BANK
25 MAIN STREET
FINSTER, OHIO

Marvin Schmeer

89" ⑆02146695⑈23010 3⑆05

MARVIN SCHMEER
FLOSSIE SCHMEER
41 ELM STREET
FINSTER, OHIO

No. 307

Mar 9 19 75

77-334
552

PAY TO THE ORDER OF _Warner's Sod Grass Supply_ $ 89.75

Eighty Nine and 75/100 ———————— DOLLARS

FIRST NATIONAL BANK
25 MAIN STREET
FINSTER, OHIO

Marvin Schmeer

89⑈ ⑆0214 6669 5⑈ 230 10 3⑆05

MARVIN SCHMEER
FLOSSIE SCHMEER
41 ELM STREET
FINSTER, OHIO

No. 328

Apr 2 19 75

77-334
552

PAY TO THE ORDER OF _J. & H. Tree Surgeons_ $ 76.55

Seventy-Six and 55/100 ———————— DOLLARS

FIRST NATIONAL BANK
25 MAIN STREET
FINSTER, OHIO

Marvin Schmeer

89⑈ ⑆0214 6669 5⑈ 230 10 3⑆05

MARVIN SCHMEER
FLOSSIE SCHMEER
41 ELM STREET
FINSTER, OHIO

No. 340

Apr. 27 19 75

77-334
552

PAY TO THE ORDER OF _Tuff-Train Obedience School_ $ 185.00

One Hundred Eighty Five and 00/100 DOLLARS

FIRST NATIONAL BANK
25 MAIN STREET
FINSTER, OHIO

Marvin Schmeer

89⑈ ⑆0214 6669 5⑈ 230 10 3⑆05

MARVIN SCHMEER
FLOSSIE SCHMEER
41 ELM STREET
FINSTER, OHIO

No. 364

May 19 19 75

77-334
552

PAY TO THE
ORDER OF Eldon Smith M.D. $ 60.00

Sixty and 0%100 _____ DOLLARS

FIRST NATIONAL BANK
25 MAIN STREET
FINSTER, OHIO

Marvin Schmeer

⑈ ⑈:0 2 ⑊ 4 6 6 9 5 ⑈ 2 3 0 ⑊ 0 3 ⑈:0 5

MARVIN SCHMEER
FLOSSIE SCHMEER
41 ELM STREET
FINSTER, OHIO

No. 365

May 20 19 75

77-334
552

PAY TO THE
ORDER OF Tuff-Train Obedience School $ 185.00

One Hundred Eighty-Five and 00/100 DOLLARS

FIRST NATIONAL BANK
25 MAIN STREET
FINSTER, OHIO

Marvin Schmeer

3 9 ⑈ :0 2 ⑊ 4 6 6 9 5 ⑈ 2 3 0 ⑊ 0 3 ⑈:0 5

MARVIN SCHMEER
FLOSSIE SCHMEER
41 ELM STREET
FINSTER, OHIO

No. 386

Jun 29 19 75

77-334
552

PAY TO THE
ORDER OF Grigsby Upholstery $ 160.00

One Hundred Sixty and 0%100 _____ DOLLARS

FIRST NATIONAL BANK
25 MAIN STREET
FINSTER, OHIO

Marvin Schmeer

⑈ :0 2 ⑊ 4 6 6 9 5 ⑈ 2 3 0 ⑊ 0 3 ⑈:0 5

MARVIN SCHMEER
FLOSSIE SCHMEER
41 ELM STREET
FINSTER, OHIO

No. 392

July 7 19 75

77-334
552

PAY TO THE ORDER OF Mike's T.V. Repair $ 85.55

Eighty-Five and 55/100 ———— DOLLARS

FIRST NATIONAL BANK
25 MAIN STREET
FINSTER, OHIO

Marvin Schmeer

89" ⑈021 46695⑈ 23010 3":05

MARVIN SCHMEER
FLOSSIE SCHMEER
41 ELM STREET
FINSTER, OHIO

No. 419

July 29 19 75

77-334
552

PAY TO THE ORDER OF Olsen's Carpet Shop $ 714.41

Seven Hundred Fourteen and 41/100 DOLLARS

FIRST NATIONAL BANK
25 MAIN STREET
FINSTER, OHIO

Marvin Schmeer

89" ⑈021 46695⑈ 23010 3":05

MARVIN SCHMEER
FLOSSIE SCHMEER
41 ELM STREET
FINSTER, OHIO

No. 427

Aug 18 19 75

77-334
552

PAY TO THE ORDER OF Century Window Glass Co. $ 104.57

One Hundred Four and 57/100 ———— DOLLARS

FIRST NATIONAL BANK
25 MAIN STREET
FINSTER, OHIO

Marvin Schmeer

89" ⑈021 46695⑈ 23010 3":05

MARVIN SCHMEER
FLOSSIE SCHMEER
41 ELM STREET
FINSTER, OHIO

No. 441

Sept. 10 19 75

77-334
552

Pay to the
Order of Hogan's Movers

$ 250.00

Two Hundred Fifty and 00/100 _____ DOLLARS

FIRST NATIONAL BANK
25 MAIN STREET
FINSTER, OHIO

Marvin Schmeer

⑈ ⑈021 46695⑈ 230103⑈05

MARVIN SCHMEER
APT. 18-A
976 LOGAN STREET
FINSTER, OHIO

No. 003

Sept. 20 19 75

77-334
552

Pay to the
Order of J. R. Bryce, Attorney at Law $ 1200.00

Twelve Hundred and 00/100 _____ DOLLARS

FIRST NATIONAL BANK
25 MAIN STREET
FINSTER, OHIO

Marvin Schmeer

⑈466989 ⑈0210⑈0055⑈ 103⑈

MARVIN SCHMEER
APT. 18-A
976 LOGAN STREET
FINSTER, OHIO

No. 009

Sept. 29 19 75

77-334
552

Pay to the
Order of Flossie Schmeer

$ 25,000.00

Twenty Five Thousand and 00/100 ___ DOLLARS

FIRST NATIONAL BANK
25 MAIN STREET
FINSTER, OHIO

Marvin Schmeer

⑈66989 ⑈0210⑈0055⑈ 103⑈

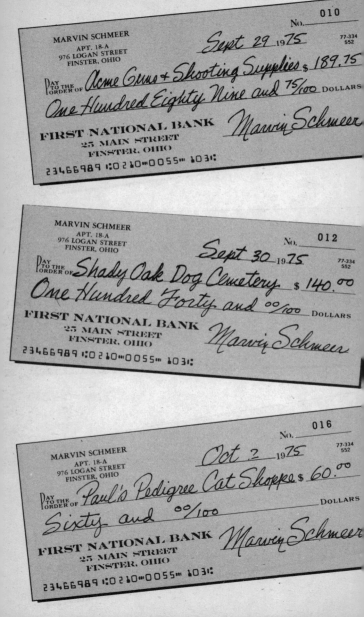

MARVIN SCHMEER
APT. 18-A
976 LOGAN STREET
FINSTER, OHIO

No. 010

77-334
552

Sept 29 19 75

PAY TO THE ORDER OF Acme Guns + Shooting Supplies $ 189.75

One Hundred Eighty Nine and 75/100 DOLLARS

FIRST NATIONAL BANK
25 MAIN STREET
FINSTER, OHIO

Marvin Schmeer

23466989 1:0210m0055m 103:

MARVIN SCHMEER
APT. 18-A
976 LOGAN STREET
FINSTER, OHIO

No. 012

77-334
552

Sept 30 19 75

PAY TO THE ORDER OF Shady Oak Dog Cemetery $ 140.00

One Hundred Forty and 00/100 DOLLARS

FIRST NATIONAL BANK
25 MAIN STREET
FINSTER, OHIO

Marvin Schmeer

23466989 1:0210m0055m 103:

No. 016

77-334
552

MARVIN SCHMEER
APT. 18-A
976 LOGAN STREET
FINSTER, OHIO

Oct 2 19 75

PAY TO THE ORDER OF Paul's Pedigree Cat Shoppe $ 60.00

Sixty and 00/100 DOLLARS

FIRST NATIONAL BANK
25 MAIN STREET
FINSTER, OHIO

Marvin Schmeer

23466989 1:0210m0055m 103:

MAD

VISITS A

STOCK

BROKER'S

OFFICE

FIGHT, TEAM, FIGHT!

!!!%↙↘:"$][!?....

163

ITT 42½   GE 17⅝   ITT 43⅛

I think
we've finally got
a bull market!

REMEMBER...PEARL...HARB

Looks like they're still getting hurt by those Japanese imports!

18¾   ITT   45¼   GE   19   OLE!

165

IBM 405½ IBM 407½ THAT'S

Now that's a **real** glamour stock!

5½ [GASP] ITT 45⅝ [WHEEZE]

166

167

169

INS👁OMNIA

REGR

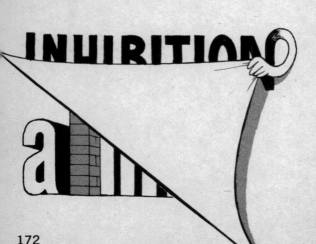

INHIBITION

a

ESSI*ON*

IMPOTENCE

TOKENI

SM

omerate

W L

KOUT A

ʎOGA

HEART

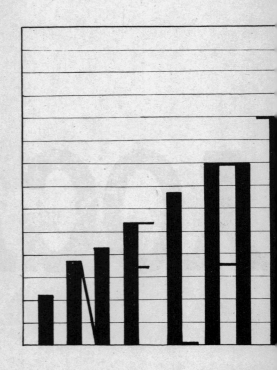

RANSPLANT

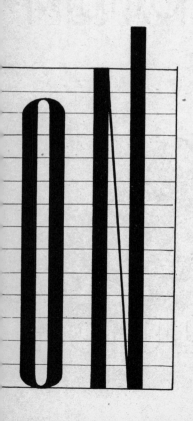

ALCOHOLISM

Pollution

DISTINCTIVE

JOHNS

in a mafia bar

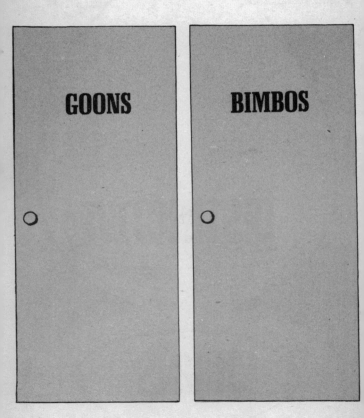

in a gay bar

HIS

His

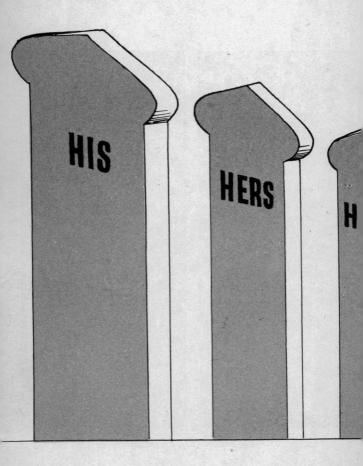

in a sheik's palace

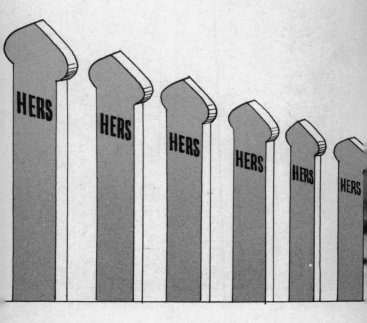

in the home of a liberated woman

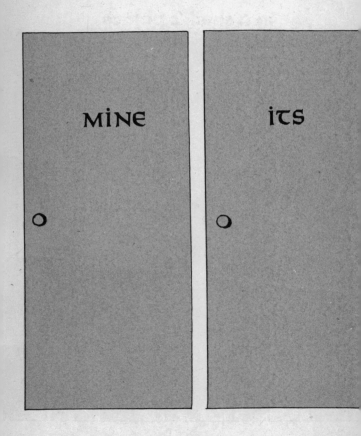

in a commune

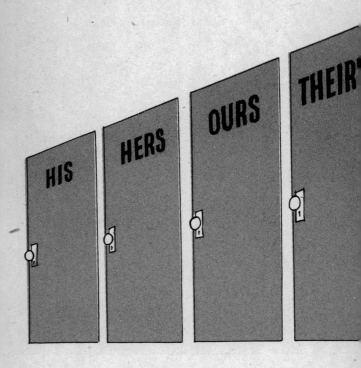

ANYONE'S EVERYBODY'S